Over the Top

Philadelphia Power series

Susan Scott Shelley
and Chantal Mer

Shelley and Mer

Chapter One

♥

Calder

Conversation and laughter fill my apartment, a drastic change from the disappointment that's hung heavy in the week since our team lost a heartbreaker of a game seven to our division rivals, forcing our exit from the hockey championship playoffs in the second round.

My teammates Leif, Axel, and Sawyer are huddled with me around my kitchen island, looking through the nominations for the upcoming hockey awards on Leif's phone with our friend Ryder, who brings the team's mascot to life. The announcements rolled out this morning, giving us a reason to celebrate.

"Calder." Leif lifts his beer, the brew nearly the same ginger red as his hair, in toast. "Congrats, kid. I'm damn proud of you."

Axel, our team captain, nods, then adjusts the sling supporting his broken arm. He played with a fractured elbow for the final two games of the series, in addition to an injured knee. "So proud. Our own Rookie of the Year."

"It's a nomination, not a win." My chiming phone interrupts me. I grab it and scan the new message.

Riggs: ETA twenty minutes.

The flutter in my chest that happens every time I think about the sexy fashion designer flairs to life. My nomination was an opportunity to reach out and ask him to dress me for the awards show. Now that the season is over, I have time to relax. Time to give into fun. Into flirting. Time to test the waters with Riggs.

"Not yet," Sawyer says with a lazy smile. He arrived here straight from his yoga class. I'd never seen yoga pants with flames racing up the sides, but our starting goalie rocks them. "Though I think you and Leif will win."

"Leif will, for sure." Willing myself to settle, I place my phone on the island then raise my glass to salute Leif. "He's the best defenseman in the league. And you should too, Sawyer. All the work you do for dogs."

"Dog dad, through and through." Ryder tips his beer in a toast to Sawyer. Sawyer's nomination for contributions to the community is well deserved.

Sawyer shrugs. "If my nomination gets more dogs adopted, that's enough of a win for me. Zeus would probably try to eat the trophy anyway."

I'm more proud of their nominations than I am for myself. Though after a full season of busting my ass, striving to exceed the expectations I had of myself and the Philadelphia Power organization had of me, getting the official word that I'm named a candidate for Rookie of the Year is gratifying.

Leif pulls me into a hug. "You worked hard. The battle for top spot among rookie goal scorers went back and forth between you and Zagras all season."

"And yet we ended up with a tie." I shake my head. Having to see Brock Zagras at the awards show is the only downer.

This entire season, the constant comparison of our stats from reporters and commentators kept our names linked day after day, a flashing reminder of our decade-long friendship, its blindsiding end a few years ago, and the animosity that's reigned in its place.

Axel shoots a coaster rolling down the island, aiming for me. Sawyer snaps his hand out, slaps the disc flat, and they both grin at each other. "As long as you don't haul off and punch his face at the show, you'll be good."

I groan, pinching the bridge of my nose. Video of me plowing my fist into his face during game three of the playoffs first round went viral. "What was I supposed to do when he took that cheap shot at your knee? Let it go?"

Sawyer pats me on the head, similar to how he pets his dog when the giant beast performs a trick well. "No. You did good. Always protect your teammates."

"Calder does better for us when he's on the ice, not sitting in the penalty box or worse, lost to us for an entire playoff game because of his actions." Blue eyes edging toward annoyance, Axel folds his arms over his chest.

"That was *one* time. And I had fewer penalties this season than you." I keep my tone mild and sweet because I don't want anything to overshadow our celebratory mood, though I'm still frustrated about that suspension. "Even with me missing the one game, we still won that series."

Better still, we kicked out Brock's team, not that it matters now since we're sitting home while the remaining teams play on.

"You always say no one hurts one of our guys and gets away with it," Ryder reminds Axel with a raised brow.

Axel sighs. "I know I do. I mean it. And I'm grateful he had my back. Just, damn it, I don't want that one action to come back and bite him in the ass during the voting."

The few sips of beer I've taken sour in my stomach. He's right. No other rookie got suspended. I don't know if the voters will count that against me. "Maybe I should've held onto my temper. But the ref ignored what Brock did, and I couldn't just skate by, pretending it was okay."

Leif shakes his head and lays a comforting hand on my shoulder. "Don't worry about that. I was proud of you for protecting your captain. Plenty of people feel the same."

"I know. But other people said I should've stuck to the game plan, tried to score, and let that be our revenge. I see their point, but if I had the chance to do it over again, I'd make the same choice." Looking at Leif, I can't be anything but honest.

Careful of his sling, Axel wraps his good arm around me. "Maybe keep that part to yourself if you're asked about it in any interviews leading up to the ceremony."

"Thanks, dude." I deadpan. "I don't know what I'd do without having you to dispense advice like that."

"Ass." Snickering, he steals my beer. He'll be at the show too, as a presenter, and I'm so glad I'll have my friends there with me.

His eye roll at Axel falling short of frustration thanks to the smile tipping up his lips, Leif opens the refrigerator and snags another beer. He twists off the cap, then hands me the fresh bottle. "Is Riggs on his way?"

I take it with an appreciative nod. Leif's always looking out for me. "Yeah. Probably fifteen minutes out."

Leif's final fitting is today, but I'm just getting started. He casts me an amused glance. "You know, you could've ordered your suit at the end of the regular season, like I did. That would've given you seven additional weeks and eliminated this last-minute rush."

"We were focused on the playoffs. I didn't have time for distractions like selecting suit options." Grumbling, I pick at the bottle's label. At Ryder's smirk and Axel's snort, I realize the words could be taken like I'm accusing Leif of not focusing enough on hockey, and that couldn't be further from the truth. "I'm not saying you were distracted. You weren't. You're always a million percent committed to being Super Dad, Super Boyfriend, Super Defenseman, and Super Alternate Captain."

His smile, which grew bigger with each rushed word of my explanation, widens into a full-blown grin. "Thanks. I can't wait to tell Jalen I've reached Super Boyfriend status."

"I'm sure he'd agree." Relief he's not annoyed relaxes the tension tightening my stomach.

Axel bumps his shoulder into mine. "Do I get to be Super Captain too?"

"Sure. If you make me iced coffee when I come visit, like Leif does."

"Dude. I gave you a coffee machine." He points to the gleaming appliance on my counter. "It literally does the job for you."

I shrug. "Leif serves his coffee in fun mugs and teaches me how to swear in Swedish."

Laughter bursts out of Leif, Ryder, and Sawyer. Giving Axel a pat on the shoulder, Sawyer whispers something I can't make out.

"Now I know what the holiday gift for everyone will be next season." Axel's smile is sharp, mischievous, and I worry I'll regret whatever he's cooking up. "Fun mugs and language learning courses. I'll tell the guys it was your idea, Cal. Much better than the gaming systems I'd been considering."

"Damn it. They'll give me shit for that. Okay, fine, you can be Super Captain too."

"Glad you see reason, rookie. Oops, can't call you that anymore." He ruffles my hair, the movement less smooth than usual since he has to use his other arm.

I may joke that Leif is my team dad, but these four looked out for me this season. I hope I've proven I have their backs too. Philly's been an amazing fit. I've found a family in the guys currently standing in my kitchen.

A knock at my front door kicks my stomach into my chest. I thrust my beer at Ryder and rush to the door. My hand shakes on the knob. Sucking in a breath, I take one last glance at my blue tee and jeans and open the door.

My heart catches at the sight of Riggs, tall, lean, and sexy in a navy blue suit with white pinstripes, a bright pink button-down shirt, and a vest in an intricate pattern of pink and blue. A tape measure is draped around his shoulders. His brown hair is short on the sides and back, and the longer curls on top are artfully tousled. I've never seen him look anything but polished and put together. My fingers and lips itch to trace over him and see how he looks all rumpled.

"Hi, Riggs. Welcome."

"Calder." Holding two suit bags over his shoulder and a binder with fabric samples tucked under his other arm, he gives me a nod. "Congratulations are in order. Well done, both you and Leif."

"Thanks. Come in." I take the suit bags from him and gesture for him to enter, wondering what Riggs will think of my apartment.

He works out of his apartment and goes to clients for fittings, so I've never seen his space. The two fittings I had with him were up in Leif's place since Leif was getting things at the same time, and our schedule was so packed at the start of the season.

"Everyone's in the kitchen and living room. Go straight down the hall." I follow him and the sound of my friends' voices, gazing at Riggs' graceful form. He carries himself so well. I'm not positive of his age, but I'd place him close to my own, twenty-two.

He greets Leif, and Leif introduces him to the others. I catch up as Riggs is offering his congratulations to Leif.

"Thank you." Leif shakes his hand. "And thanks for handling us both at the same time today."

"You two living in the same building is convenient." Riggs takes both bags from me and gives one to Leif. "This one is yours."

The bag rustles with Leif's long strides. Pausing outside my bedroom, he raises his eyebrows at me. "I'll change in here."

"Don't worry, there shouldn't be any surprises for you to find," I call after him, and he laughs as he cautiously pushes the door open with his foot.

Ryder taps the back of my head as he passes me. "Dude, that was a wild night."

Sawyer waggles his brows at me. "*Wild* is the right word."

Heat flames into my cheeks at Riggs' interested slow blink. Now, I wish I had a better story to tell. "Sawyer, why don't you make Riggs some coffee?"

"Riggs, do you want coffee? We also have beer." Sitting on a stool at the island beside Sawyer, Axel pipes up, happy to play host in my home. "Calder has sports drinks and protein shakes too."

Riggs tears his curious gaze from me and gives Axel a smile. "Coffee would be wonderful, thank you."

Axel taps Sawyer on the chest and points him to the coffeemaker. I lose interest in my friends' jostling each other as Riggs lays the bag on my couch before placing the binder on the coffee table.

When he turns back to me, curiosity still haunts his gaze. "I want to hear that story. From Sawyer's insinuation, it sounds scandalous."

He's standing close enough that I could reach out and touch him. Resisting the temptation is tough when I'm fighting against a magnetic pull. "Unfortunately, it was *wild* in terms of wildlife. Urban wildlife. A squirrel got in my bedroom from a hole it clawed through a wall in the closet. It dashed out of the bedroom, almost ran into Leif as it raced into the living room. These guys were all here. We corralled it in the bathroom and had to call animal control."

His lips quirk into a smile and his eyes fill with mirth. "A wild night indeed."

My body is reacting to his scent, his nearness, and the music that is his voice, and I need to get things back on track. Depending on Riggs' schedule, custom suits can take anywhere from two weeks to twelve weeks. When I texted him this morning, he assured me he could accommodate my tight timeframe. "Thanks for fitting me in with such short notice."

"Anything for my favorite client." The shine in his eyes softens. He lifts his elegant fingers and trails them over the bare skin of my forearm. There's a spark. One we both feel from the way his surprised gaze jumps to meet mine. Goosebumps rise amid the flash of heat. The touch is gone too soon.

Craving more, I shift a step closer and wonder if he can hear how hard my heart is beating. I could get lost in those eyes. "You probably say that to all your clients."

His gaze journeys over my face, and I look my fill, cataloging every tiny freckle and the way his lashes fan out, framing his hazel eyes. He leans in so his words carry solely to my ears. "Only the ones with piercing blue eyes and hair that looks like it's been kissed by moonlight."

The words leave me lightheaded and aching to hold him. Kissed by moonlight is poetic. Romantic. Words said from lips I've often thought of kissing.

"That's beautiful." I'm whispering too, and picturing him in a lush garden lit by moonlight and scented by roses, wearing one of his three piece suits. Quiet kisses and darkened corners and endless moments to spend with this spellbinding man.

I'm kicking myself now for not pursuing something with him the first time we met, at Leif's during a suit fitting before the start of the season. The pressure to give the game, and the team, my all, meant my entire focus had to be on hockey. No distractions.

But I wanted Riggs. *So much.*

That want swells fast and furious, overwhelming me as we gaze at each other in my sunny living room.

Want.

Just from talking with Riggs about clothes and my style. Well before Riggs' hands were on me to measure my chest, waist, arms, legs, seat, and thighs, though that escalated the want even more. Ordering suits was the only indulgence I allowed myself these last ten months, since I needed them for traveling to games and during road trips. He had my measurements on file, so a shirt or pants here, a pocket square there, kept the connection. I could've done the same for the awards ceremony, but I wanted, no *needed*, to see him in person.

He draws in a breath, then gives himself a shake and steps away from me. His focus darts to my friends, and he raises his voice to its usual level. "Since we only have twenty-four days until the awards show, I brought something I think would, well, suit you."

Laughing, I'm beyond pleased with how quick and witty he is and share his grin. The other three are watching us, so I try to school my features, but fail to dim my smile. "I trust you. You know what I like and what looks good."

Riggs can alter all sorts of clothes, but nothing compares to a Riggs James original. He unzips the bag. "I like that you're not afraid of color and pattern. This is one I'd already started. When I saw the material, I thought of you. It's in your preferences of style and fit. The jacket is single breasted, has notched lapels, double welted pockets, and a center vent back style."

I like that he's thinking of me when he sees material. I like that he's thinking of me in any way. The suit is a bright teal blue with a herringbone pattern. "I love it."

"Thought you might." He passes me the jacket. The inside lining is a sunny yellow with orange and green dots. "It's a silk wool blend. Lightweight and very comfortable for summer. I've brought you a white button down with teal buttons, and I know you, so no tie."

"Yeah, never a tie." The silk lining glides under my hands. "I really like the suit. The attention you paid to the shirt buttons."

His eyes light up like I've made his year by approving his choice. "The teal will look great with your eyes. When I got your text requesting a less flashy option than your usual style, I researched past awards shows and found the players tend to stick with blues and grays, so I thought this could be a good option."

I have to swallow a few times to ease the thickening in my throat. He gets me. He *sees* me. "Thank you. This blue is still different enough for me to feel like myself. You knocked this one clear out of the park, Riggs."

"Thank you." Something flickers in his eyes and the invisible tether between us reels me a step closer. Footsteps sound behind me. Riggs drags his gaze away from me at Sawyer's approach. Sawyer picks up the fabric book and Riggs assents with a wave of his hand. "Feel free to have a look. My goal is always that the clothes I make showcase the body well, both stationary and in motion. And that they tell the story the client wants to tell."

He's confident and sure, and I can't tear my gaze from him. The patter of Sawyer's footfall ceases and is followed by the sound of a barstool scraping against the kitchen floor. "You always succeed. I know I'm in good hands with you."

Behind us, one of the three in the kitchen chokes back a laugh. Wishing we didn't have an audience, I slide one hand behind my back and flip them off.

Which only gets me more laughter.

Leif comes out of the bedroom, looking good in a slim-fitting navy blue suit. The guys whistle and applaud, and I join in. He does a little spin, flashes us a grin, and walks to stand in front of Riggs and me. "It fits well."

I step back so Riggs can get on with whatever tailoring magic he needs to do with Leif. As he checks the fit, he glances at me. "I saw the press announcement, Calder. You scored the most goals and assists of all rookies."

"The most goals, most assists, *and* nineteen multi-point games. More than any other rookie," Leif interjects proudly.

"So, if you have the most points, why are there two other nominees listed? Doesn't that show you're already the best?"

Rescuing my abandoned beer and Riggs' coffee from the kitchen island, I shake my head. "Having the most points doesn't automatically mean I'll win."

Frowning, Riggs continues fussing over Leif. "Why not?"

"The hockey writers choose the award and they look at a bunch of different factors." I set his coffee on a side table at the couch's end and tick each off voting consideration on my fingers. "Total points, goals, assists, the number of games played, a player's ice time, their style of play. How a player supports their linemates, how many goals they scored on power plays and shorthanded."

"So it's on a player's overall body of work." He nods and gives Leif an approving nod. "You're all set. No further alterations needed."

"Thanks." Leif steps aside, smoothing a hand down his lapel, and claps me on the shoulder. "You're up."

"Be right back." Suit in hand, I head for my bedroom, and leave the door ajar as I dress so I can hear the conversation. Sawyer and Axel mention making appointments with Riggs for the end of summer. Leif's asking Riggs about his brother Kingston, who introduced Leif to Riggs. The suit and shirt are comfortable, fit me well, and that they were crafted by Riggs' hands gives me a charge.

Riggs' scrutiny will soon be focused on me, so I look down at my cock and will it to behave. Heartbeat pounding, I add shoes, then return to the living room, and the flutter in my chest resumes at the approval shining in Riggs' eyes.

"You look good." He summons me to his side with a wave of his hand.

Whistles and applause rise from my teammates. I give them a turn, like Leif did.

With a light touch that feels much bigger than it is, Riggs checks that the shoulder seam ends at my shoulder line, adds a couple of pins, and I draw in a lungful of his fresh scent that I want to roll around in.

He checks the jacket length. Long fingers and that tape measure touch the span of my shoulders. "Do you know the other two players nominated with you?"

I can't help sucking in a breath at the feel of his fingertips at my waist. "Brock Zagras plays for New York. We have a strong rivalry. The other nominee is Igor Vasilevski. He plays for Seattle. I don't know him personally, but I've heard he's a nice guy."

The edge of the tape measure trails along my leg as Riggs drops to a crouch to check my pant length. "Good choice on the shoes. Besides the Rookie of the Year and Leif's best defenseman, who else is voted on?"

With his head in line with my dick, concentrating on words is difficult. I will my body to behave. "The most valuable player, best goalie, best defensive forward, most goals, most points in a season, coach and GM of the year."

"Hmm." He tugs on the material around my ankles.

The brush of soft curls against the back of my fingers seizes my focus and I picture tugging those curls while his lips tease my cock. I bite the inside of my lip and force my attention back to the topic. "There are awards for sportsmanship, perseverance, leadership, humanitarian contributions, and Sawyer is up for the community contributions award."

"Congratulations, Sawyer." Riggs stands and returns the tape measure to hang around his shoulders. His cheeks have a light flush, his eyes are bright, and he sucks in a breath as he meets my gaze. "The suit needs some minor alterations."

Minor alterations means I'll get to see him again. I'm all for that. "No problem."

The calendar app on his phone is filled with dozens of colorful blocks. "I'll have this done for you by the sixteenth. Are you free that day?"

"Yeah. I'm flying home to Minneapolis to spend some time with my family, but I'll be back on the fourteenth."

"Okay, so the sixteenth, at noon?" Brows lifted, gaze so focused on mine, he parts his lips the barest bit like he's thinking about kissing me, and damn, I wish he would.

"It's a date." The words fly out, quick and eager, and heat flares up my neck. One of the trio by the kitchen island chuckles.

Ears red, Riggs drags his attention to Leif. "Leif, I'll have the final alterations on Thea's dress for your friend's wedding done then too. Can you meet at the same time? I'm sorry to double you both up again, but I have a wedding that evening and need to drive down to Stone Harbor so I can't meet later."

Leif consults his phone. "That's fine. A group appointment is always fun."

Sawyer's eyes light up, twinkling with too much mischief. "Ooh, maybe we should all come too."

The temptation to flip him off again is strong. I don't want my love life playing out in front of them like some reality dating show.

"I'm going to change." Keeping my ears pricked for whatever Sawyer and the others may say, I head to my bedroom and carefully strip off the suit then tug on my tee and jeans. I'm bummed the fitting won't be just the two of us, but Riggs doesn't have time to hang around after that appointment anyway, so it's not like I can offer to take him to lunch once we're done.

Though I could ask him now if he'd like to join me for a drink or dinner sometime. But the guys are here, and asking him in front of them isn't ideal. Debating when, where, and how to approach Riggs, I return to the living room and hand him the clothes.

Shooting me an intense look, Ryder motions for me to join him by the coffee maker. When I get there, he tugs me closer by the hem of my shirt and whispers, "You get to bring someone to the awards show."

He'll be Sawyer's plus one. I figured I'd go alone, but having Riggs there... Would he even go with me?

"Ask him." He subtly angles his head in the sexy man's direction.

Ears heating, I glance at Axel and Sawyer poking through the fabric samples, then Leif. "I don't want an audience."

"I'll take care of them." He claps me twice on the shoulder, slips something that feels like metal into my back pocket, then steps away. Patting his front pockets in an exaggerated fashion, he pulls a surprised expression. "I think I lost my keys. Hey, Axel, Sawyer, Leif, come help me. They're probably somewhere in the hall, Calder's bedroom, or the bathroom. Or up in Leif's apartment."

Rolling his eyes, Axel pushes off of his stool. "This is why you shouldn't do walking handstands all over the place."

"A mascot's got to practice." He rolls into a cartwheel, then a handstand and on those hands, with his long hair curtaining his face, he heads into the hallway.

Sawyer sets his drink down with a laugh. "Coming. I'll search the bedroom. Captain Grumpy can take the bath, and Leafy can help Ryder check the hall."

Leif gives Ryder, then me, a look suggesting he knows what's going on, and smoothly shakes Riggs' hand. "Thanks for the suit. Beautiful work, as always. If you're gone before we find these keys, I'll see you on the sixteenth."

My four friends vacate the kitchen and living room, searching my apartment for keys hidden in my back pocket. Ryder's a genius. I owe him.

Riggs' expression pinches in suspicion at their hasty exit. Then he fixes those gorgeous eyes on me. "We've never had time to talk, just the two of us."

"Nope. Leif's always been there, or it's been impersonal texts about orders." Mouth dry, my heartbeat hammering, I stroll toward him, hoping I look calmer than I feel. No idea how long we have before the others return. I need to talk fast. "I'd like to get to know you, Riggs. As more than my designer."

His sweeping stare takes my whole body in. I'm close enough now to spy the ring of brown in that grass green and the way his pupils expand. "I wouldn't turn that down."

I stand tall, striving for confidence, though the nerves needling my stomach taunt me. My hands ball into fists in my front pockets and I remind myself that I've always gone after what I want and I'm not about to stop now. "How about we get to know each other better in New York? Will you be my date to the awards show?"

His eyes widen. "You want me to go with you? Awards shows are events for someone special, not a first date with a stranger."

"We're not strangers." I give him my best smile, but seduction is probably tempered by my eagerness. "Strangers wouldn't know my inseam size."

He barks out a laugh. "Touché."

I remember Leif saying that Riggs wanted to grow his business among athletes. "The room will be filled with hockey players, so going is a good business opportunity for you."

He tips his head to the side, studying me. "That is true."

"And I'll be a walking advertisement for you." I gesture at the suit bag.

Narrowing his eyes, he wraps the end of the measuring tape around his wrist. "You're doing an awful lot of work to convince me to go. Are these shows numbingly boring or something?"

"I've never been, but I don't think so. Leif says the bar is always well-stocked and the food is good. The hotel is nice too. We can go up the day before the show. There's a reception for the nominees Friday night at eight, but we don't have to stay long. We can check out some restaurants, go sightseeing. Visit the garment district. Whatever you want. The show is Saturday night. We'll come back to Philly on Sunday."

"So a weekend away." His voice lowers and his smile slowly builds. "That's a big deal first date. With several costume changes. Will we be sharing a hotel room?"

"Uh." I hadn't thought that far ahead. "We can? I booked my room this morning. It has two queen beds. I'll see if there's another available and book it for you."

He rests his elegant fingers on my forearm. "I don't mind sharing a room with you. Though don't go telling everyone I offer that as part of my tailoring services."

"Just for your favorite client?" I tease.

Those fingertips flex in the faintest strokes before falling away. "Yes, Calder, just for you."

Footsteps precede Axel's entry into the room. He shrugs his shoulders at us. "They're not in the bathroom."

Riggs casts a glance at his phone, its screen lighting up with notifications. "I should go. I have work to do."

"Thanks for coming over." I help him gather the bag, then carry his fabric sample book to the door. Our fingers brush when I hand it over and I close my hand tight to capture the tingling.

"Goodbye, Calder." His nod is almost regal, yet there's a longing in his features that suggests he doesn't want us to part.

"Take care, Riggs." Bringing my still tingling hand to my chest, I close the door.

An entire weekend with Riggs in New York. Time to pull out all the stops.

Chapter Two

♥

Riggs

"I still can't believe you hired a car service to bring us here." I follow Calder from the black luxury sedan, sliding along the leather seats to the door the driver is holding open. The summer heat of NYC is a smack in the face after two hours in a climate-controlled car sipping mimosas.

Calder says something I can't make out to the driver, then clasps my hand. "It beats driving with my rowdy teammates or taking the train."

"Really?" In front of us, with its glass facade, highlighted by a fire-red door surround and accents, stands The Museum at FIT. I let out a breath and squeeze his hand, my excitement like hundreds of champagne bubbles fizzing in my stomach. "You're not close with Leif, Axel, and Sawyer?"

"And Ryder. I am. They're great." He leads me to the museum. A hint of citrus and freshness float on the air, engulfing me like the softest chenille. "My transition would have been a lot harder without them, especially Leif. But... I wanted to have time with just you." He waves to a bored looking security guard who lumbers forward.

A pleasant heat surges up the back of my neck. "Is that so?"

"It is." His lips spread into a *U*, highlighting the divot in his chin. "Are you going to answer everything I say with a question?"

I press my torso into his muscular arm. "Would that bother you?"

"Can I help you?" The security guard's broad body takes up the three feet he's cracked open the door as he looks us over.

With a full wattage smile, Calder holds up his phone. "I was in contact with Juliet about a private viewing of the Dior and Balenciaga exhibit. I'm–"

"Calder MacKinnon. Up for Rookie of the Year." The guard steps back and holds the door open as we pass through. "If I weren't a born and bred New Yorker, I'd say I was rooting for you. But I *am* a New Yorker, so I gotta go with my boy, Brock."

Calder flashes a gracious grin, but the tips of his ears turn the same shade of pink as the stripes on his shirt. That he's shocked to be recognized is adorable and makes him even more endearing. "Nice to know if I ever move to New York, I'll have a fan."

The guard chuckles and points us toward the exhibit. "When you're done, you can check out the Gallery FIT, but you'll have to stay out of the Fashion and Textile History Gallery because that's where they're filming the documentary."

"Thanks." Calder shakes the guard's hand and I wave as we head toward the exhibit. "I like your voice, so no."

I cock my head back. "What are you talking about?"

"You wanted to know if you'd bother me answering everything with a question. No, because I like your voice. Plus, being alone with you is something I've wanted for a long time." He's close enough, the coarse hair on his forearm tickles my skin and I lick my lips.

The instant I met Calder at Leif's condo, I was taken with him. Not just for his gorgeous blue eyes, dark like the deepest depths of the ocean. It was his sweet nature, as is evident by the fact that even though the museum is closed today, we're standing in front of gorgeous gowns designed by two of the most influential couturiers of our time. He pulled strings because he thought this was something I'd enjoy.

Though, seeing his athletic pants hug his buttocks as he laid on the floor coloring a picture of a bunny family cooking with Leif's daughter Thea was also quite alluring.

I straighten the crease on my vintage Yeossal trousers. Now is not the time to contemplate the perfect bubble of Calder's bottom. "I'm quite pleased you decided on the car service."

"Yeah?" Fingertips dance along my skin. The touch is so light, were I not attuned to him, I might have missed it. The gentleness contradicts the fierce player I've watched on the ice.

I bump his shoulder. "Now who's answering with a question?"

"You." Husky voice a whisper, he dips his head. "What do you think?"

Heated breath teases my ear, sending a delicious shiver cascading down my spine. All thoughts zero in on licking the divot in his chin, but I push them away. "I believe this is the first time Dior and Balenciaga designs have been exhibited side-by-side." I regard the 1957 embroidered silk Dior ball gown next to the 1961 Balenciaga silk faille evening dress. Both in beige, they are elegant without being overstated. "I'm glad they have the placards. Seeing them next to each other, it's hard to know for certain who the designer is."

He shifts until the pads of his fingertips are whisking the pads of my fingers, and I shiver. "So you like it?"

"I love it. But if you get bored, tell me, and we'll leave." We move to the next grouping.

"I won't."

Tapping my chin with my finger, I inspect the black coat dress and the black two piece set and try to decipher which is the Dior. "Get bored or tell me?"

Calder grasps my hand, interrupting my mental gymnastics and kisses the knuckle of the finger I was batting my chin with. "Get bored."

"Oh." My stomach loops. His sweetness knows no bounds. "You're quite charming."

"And you're quite dashing." He dips his voice and trails his fingers along the brown suspenders I paired with the chestnut plaid pants and fitted, short-sleeved button-down shirt. "I never realized how sexy suspenders were."

The heat in his gaze as he follows the journey of his fingertips has me shifting my feet, and I can feel my own ears heating. I push up the tortoise shell glasses that have no prescriptive value, but are a crucial part of the overall aesthetic of my outfit. "I was going to wear a bow tie and wingtips, but my brother insisted it was too much for walking around New York." I lift my foot, showing off the vintage white leather Puma's I found in pristine condition at an estate auction two years ago. "So I went more casual, but now," I gesture to the gowns and dresses, "I feel underdressed."

"Nah, your brother was right. I'm not sure I'd be able to control myself with suspenders, a bow tie, *and* wingtips." He clutches my suspenders, tugging twice, then releases his hold and smooths his palm over my chest. "Let's play a game. You guess the designer, and I'll tell you if you're correct."

I chuckle at him placing his hand over the first placard, blocking it from my view. "You're on. That one is Dior."

He lifts his hand, revealing that I'm correct. "Yep."

"Do I win anything?"

"How about a kiss?" He steps closer, bracing his hand on my hip. My already heated core runs hotter. Words elude me and I nod, then his lips touch mine. A brush of softness and heat that tastes of mint and leaves my lips tingling and me yearning for more.

"I like this game."

We spend the next hour exploring the work of two geniuses. Every time I'm correct, Calder cheers and kisses me. And for every incorrect answer, he pokes out his bottom lip, making a buzzer sound, but I still get a kiss, so it isn't a total loss.

"How'd you get into tailoring?"

I consider his question. No one has asked me that before. Perhaps it's because of my social media presence, people think they know the answer. "I always enjoyed making things. Kingston—"

"Your brother, right?"

"Yes. He was involved in theater when he was in high school, and he'd bring me with him." When I look back on that time, it was remarkable Kingston didn't let babysitting his baby brother interfere with his extracurricular activities. "I was only six or seven and became the theater group's mascot. As I got older, I went from being a gopher to helping paint sets. The girl who did the costumes showed me how to sew, and I excelled at it. Kingston said I had a good eye, and before long, I was making recommendations about costumes and sketching designs."

"The sewing tutorials you've posted online are great," he says.

My chest flutters. I can't believe he's watched my sewing videos. Though, I suppose it's not any stranger than me taking a sudden liking to hockey. "Thanks."

We explore the rest of the museum, getting to know each other with stories from Calder about growing up with a pro-hockey player as a dad, and how he's never wanted to do anything else, and me telling him about the evolution of my business. It's a typical first date conversation, but there's an ease that was not typical during any of my previous first dates. Perhaps it's because we've worked together for the last ten months and already have a rapport. Or perhaps it's because Calder is one of those people who makes everyone feel like they are the most interesting person he's ever met.

By the time we finish, I'm tucked next to Calder. My cheeks are tired from smiling so much. He texts our driver, then slips the phone back into his pocket. "I liked the Balenciaga green and yellow gown best. The colors, the pattern. Very cool."

The pattern and silk taffeta of the printed evening gown were very 1961 but would be stunning on any red carpet today. I love that even if this isn't his thing; Calder seemed to have fun. "You and your color."

"Life's too short to wear boring clothes." He bumps our hips together. "You taught me that."

I loop my arm through his. When you're a ten-year-old boy who loves sewing and fashion, you become the butt of jokes, and learn quickly that people can be wankers. Having Calder appreciate what I do and understand my passion leaves me unsteady. "You're sweet. Thank you for this." I rest my head on his shoulder with a contented sigh.

"My pleasure." His lips brush the top of my head. "I wanted a chance to do something fun before everything starts up. The cocktail party tonight. Interview tomorrow morning. Then the awards ceremony... I didn't want you to feel rushed through the museum."

We thank the guard, and Calder autographs a map of the museum for him before we jump into the car and head to the hotel.

We arrive at the hotel on Park Avenue, and a doorman greets us as we enter the modern art déco lobby. While Calder checks in, I take a seat on one of the plush cushioned settees clustered throughout the lobby. I run my palm over the microfiber fabric as I watch people come and go.

It's easy to pick out the hockey players who have yet to find a decent tailor. One guy's back pockets are so close together, they look like they're about to kiss. I make a mental note to find him this weekend and give him my card. There is no excuse for sloppy work like that. Maybe I should do a video series specifically for hockey players and men built like them to educate them on proportions and what to expect from an experienced tailor.

"Riggs." Leif waves as he strides from the entrance, his boyfriend Jalen at his side. "Where's Calder?"

I stand and shake their hands in greeting. "Checking in. We just arrived."

"Jay and I were out taking in the sights." He slips his hand to rest on Jalen's back.

Jalen does the same to Leif, their appreciation for each other evident in the simple gesture. "We're going to come back next month with Thea. She hasn't been to the Museum of Natural History yet."

"She'll love that. The last time I saw her, she was talking about dinosaurs." I still have the picture of the dinosaur she drew for me tucked in Leif's file, waiting for a day when I'm able to use it in a design for Leif.

"Hey guys." Calder pulls Leif into a backslapping hug and does the same with Jalen. "Good to see you."

Leif pushes Calder's shoulder. "Like you weren't at my place last night eating all my food."

"You cook. I don't. I'm providing a service so your food doesn't go to waste." He lifts his hands palms up, an adorable smile playing on his lips. "It's a win-win for everyone."

Chuckling, Leif rolls his eyes. "If that helps you sleep at night…"

"That and a full belly." Calder pats his flat stomach, then holds up two key cards and waves them at me. "You ready to check out our room?"

"Sure." My stomach swooshes. Sharing a room is the part of this date that's made me the most nervous. I know I agreed to it, but I've never shared a room with someone I'm dating so quickly. The only thing that prevented me from obsessing too much is having two beds.

"The bellman will bring up our bags." He presses his hand to my back. His fingers fan out, sending pinpoints of heat through the breathable cotton of my shirt, and says to Leif and Jalen, "See you at the cocktail reception."

Leif nods, and Jalen raises his hand as Calder directs me to the bank of elevators, palm on my lower back. His hand remains where it is through the ride up to the fifth floor and down the long corridor, where the only sound is the muffled padding of our footsteps on the thick carpet. Our room is at the end of the hallway. Calder drops his hand and presses the key card to the keypad. With a click, the green light flashes, and he swings open the door.

"This is nice. Bigger than I expected." I follow Calder, taking in the white marble foyer. Peeking into the bathroom as we pass, I note the same white marble and a walk-in shower that must be at least half the size of my entire bathroom at home. Too busy gawking at the bathroom, I plow, face first, into a wall of muscle with an *oof.* "Sorry."

Calder doesn't respond.

Unable to see around him, I scoot to his side, and my mouth goes dry. "Oh."

The tastefully neutral room with a color palette of grays, creams, and pops of moss green has a small desk with chairs on either side of it in one corner. In the other corner is a richly upholstered chair with matching ottoman, beckoning one to curl up with a nightcap and watch the city from the window that spans the entire wall. And in the middle of the room is a very large, very singular king-sized bed.

"I'll take care of this." Calder strides to the in-room phone. "I promise, my room reservation was for two queens." He picks up the phone and punches a button. "I wouldn't—" Like he's afraid I'm going to bolt, he keeps his gaze glued to me while he speaks to the person on the other end of the phone, requesting another room, asking for a cot, then acquiescing.

His concern for my comfort is sweet, but I also know the hotel is booked solid. Between the people staying here for the awards ceremony and a wedding, they are at capacity.

He sets the phone in the cradle and releases a sigh. "There aren't any extra rooms, but they're giving us a hundred dollar food and beverage credit to use while we're here." He pinches the bridge of his nose, his jaw ticking with every clench. "I can get you a room in another hotel. Or you can stay here and I'll go to another hotel."

"It's fine." I go to him and place my hand on his chest. "We'll make do."

Those big hands grip my hips, and he dips his forehead to mine. "I don't want you to be uncomfortable. To think I planned this."

"We're good." I press my mouth to his lips, intending to reassure him. This isn't the same as the short, playful kisses at the museum. I jolt at the charge that electrifies me when our lips touch. His hold grounds me from being catapulted across the room.

His grip, the sweep of his tongue seeking entry, the rush of blood pulsing through my veins are all the permission needed to let go. I release control and immerse myself in the sensations of muscled arms engulfing me and the soft stroke of fingertips gliding over my throat. His hard rod pressed against my hipbone, and the brush of our tongues is a greater high than finding an Armani tuxedo in a pile of junk at a thrift store.

He thrusts his hip into my eager cock, and I moan into his mouth. I feel his smile, and he does it again. Fisting the fabric of his shirt, I shift my hips and grind our dicks together.

"Fuck." He breaks the kiss, his hand palming the back of my neck. Our chests rise and fall in sync. "That was…"

I straighten my glasses. "Unexpected?"

"Nah. I always knew kissing you would be mind-blowing." Keeping our bodies close, he massages my neck. "That's why I waited so long to ask you out. I knew one kiss, and I'd lose my focus."

A thrill surges through me at his words. "And now? You're not concerned about your focus?"

"Now, the season's over and I have time to recalibrate." He presses his lips to the skin just behind my ear, and I shiver. "A summer to acclimate myself to your mouth."

Laughter flares in my chest and I push at him, but he keeps me in his grip, beautiful eyes skating over my face like he's memorizing my features.

A knock at the door interrupts the moment. Calder releases me to answer it and directs the bellhop on where to put our luggage before tipping him and closing the door.

"You know," he tucks his hands into his pockets and strolls toward me, "we could skip the cocktail party."

I shake my head. "I will not be responsible for your lack of focus this soon into our date."

He tugs me to him. "Fine, but we're not staying there long."

"That's a reasonable compromise." And I press my lips to the divot that's teased me all day.

·❤·❤·❤·❤·❤·

The square bar off the lobby seats forty easily, and every one of the bar stools is occupied. The connected restaurant is closed to the public for the event and small groups relax at round tables while waitstaff in black pants and vests with crisp white shirts traverse the area with trays of hors d'oeuvres. Everything from littleneck clams with breadcrumbs to miniature gourmet grilled cheese on sourdough bread to an array of olives in shot glasses passes by us.

"I see Sawyer and Ryder." Calder points to the end of the bar where the two men are chatting with a small group. He takes a breath, smoothing down the front of his pink floral jacket, and for the first time, I realize how nervous he is. "Do I look okay?"

I straighten his black lapels, if only as an excuse to touch him. "Would I allow you to leave the room looking anything less than magnificent?"

The pinch between his brows eases and the corner of his mouth tics up. "I like magnificent." His gaze roams my form. "Did you ask me what I was wearing so you could coordinate your outfit to mine?"

"You know the answer." I adjust the front of his white shirt so the buttons line up with the button of his black slim-fit trousers. My orchid suit jacket has the faintest threads of pink weaved through it. The gray brocade shirt is a nod to Calder's jacquard jacket, and my gray Soho trousers keep us from looking too planned, while preserving the attention on Calder's outfit. "Clashing was never an option."

"Thank you." He brushes his lips across my cheek with the faintest kiss. Maybe I should have agreed to skipping the cocktail party. Not making use of the enormous bed right now seems like a missed opportunity.

Threading our fingers together, he leads me through the crowd, stopping to engage in pleasantries and introducing me to other players, sports journalists, coaches, and spouses. After thirty minutes, I've lost sight of Sawyer and Ryder.

"MacKinnon." A guy in an uninspired navy suit with an equally uninspired tie weaves through the crowd. He's wearing a grin as welcoming as a snarl.

Calder's grip on my hand tightens, his muscles stiffening the closer the dark-haired man gets. "You don't like him?"

Eyes fixed on the target approaching us, his jaw ticks and jumps. "We're up for the same award."

"He could use a stylist." I don't point out that he hasn't answered my question. My job as his escort is to reduce his stress level, not increase it.

As I intended, he huffs a laugh and his muscles relax a smidgen as the man reaches us.

"Brock," Calder says with all the enthusiasm of me at a sporting event.

The Brock fellow gestures around the room. "Can you believe this?"

"We're fortunate." Calder releases my hand and wraps his arm around my waist. "Brock Zagaras, this is my date, Riggs James."

When Brock meets my gaze, some of the tension in his expression eases. "It's a pleasure." Returning his attention to Calder, he zeroes in on Calder's outfit. "I like your jacket. Where'd you get it?"

"I made it." I nod thanks to the waiter bringing Calder and me the drinks we ordered ten minutes ago and take my strawberry Manhattan, which is supposed to be one of the hotel's signature drinks.

Brock's eyes widen. "Really?"

"Riggs is the best tailor anywhere." Calder looks at me with pride as he sips his piscoteque with lemon. "He makes a lot of my suits and shirts, and he's been dressing Leif and some of the other guys on the team for a couple of years." Calder holds an arm out. "You won't find this quality anywhere else."

Brock rubs the fabric of Calder's sleeve between his fingers, then looks down at his own humdrum suit. "Wow."

"I'm glad to catch you two." The baritone voice behind us is soft and accented, and reminds me of the Russian model I dressed during Philly Fashion Week a few years ago.

Calder and I turn simultaneously toward the voice's owner. He's the person with the dreadful tailoring I spotted in the lobby earlier today. The urge to inspect his backside pocket placement is great, but I curb it.

"Igor." Calder holds out his hand and Igor takes it, pulling him into a backslapping hug.

"It's good to meet you for real." The massive man stands several inches above Calder and Brock, but his energy is of a young pup who views everyone as his new best friend. "I can't believe we're here." He dips his head. "We're in the same room as Leif Larsson."

The awe in his voice is charming, and I remember Calder telling me that Igor is a defenseman, like Leif. I like the way Calder takes my hand when he says, "Igor Vasilevski, this is Riggs James—"

"The best tailor anywhere," Brock finishes, a challenge in his smirk. "He makes Calder's suits."

"You make suits?" Either unaware or ignoring the lasers Brock and Calder are shooting at each other, Igor pins me with his full attention. "How expensive is it?"

"Having worked in community theater where the coffee budget is more than the costume budget, I can work within most economic constraints." Hoping to interrupt the stare down between Calder and Brock, I tug on Calder's hand.

It doesn't work.

"Can I see your pants?" Igor's request unlocks Calder and Brock's battling glares, and he twirls his finger over Calder's head, indicating he should turn. "Lift your jacket—which is awesome, by the way—and let me see your pockets."

Brock stops one of the traveling waitstaff and picks several figs in a flakey pastry. "Yeah, MacKinnon. Show us your ass."

Calder opens his mouth like he's ready to let Brock have it, but I quiet him with a hand on his shoulder. "Please."

He snaps his mouth shut and turns so his back is to us. I lift his jacket and bite back a moan at the gorgeous bubble butt, beautifully showcased in perfectly fitted pants. "I've learned that many of you hockey players have the same problem." Like I'm teaching an anatomy class, I point to Calder's thighs, then that glorious bottom. "Your legs, specifically your thighs and bottoms, are disproportionately larger than your waists, which is great for speed and power on the ice, but makes purchasing pants problematic."

"Yes." Igor spins around, lifting his jacket at the same time. "I have to buy two sizes up, but then my ass looks like this."

"Dude." Brock drops his blanketed fig onto his plate. "Why do your pockets look like that?"

Igor looks over his shoulder at us, his expression a mixture of amusement and distress. "I don't know!"

I let Calder's jacket fall over his backside, quietly mourning its absence, and he turns, then bends to get a better view of Igor's pants. "It's like they're growing out of your crack."

"Cover up." Brock holds his hand in front of his eyes. "No one wants to see that."

Fighting his laughter, Calder bites his bottom lip, and for the first time since Brock approached us, the two look like they could be friends.

"This is what I'm saying. How do I fix this?" Igor waves his hand in big circles around his bottom.

"Riggs will hook you up." Calder trails a hand between my shoulder blades and I lean into his touch. "While you straighten Igor out, I'll get us some food. Want a little of everything?"

I brush my knuckle along the outside of his thigh. "Please."

"You know, the wait staff will come to you." Brock holds up his plate, and his tone has an edge of snark in it.

"They're congregating in the restaurant area and I don't want Riggs to wait any longer." The way they're snarling at each other, I wouldn't be surprised if one or both started throwing punches, recreating their fight from the playoffs. "Back soon." Calder kisses my cheek and strolls to the bar, stopping to talk and take pictures with people vying for his attention along the way.

Igor's enormous hand on my forearm steals my attention from my gorgeous date. "You can help me?"

"Yes." I remove the silver-plated business card holder Kingston gifted me for my eighteenth birthday from my interior pocket and hand the men cards. "Where are you located?"

Igor reads the card, then tucks it into his jacket pocket. "I'm on the west coast, but I'll come to your shop."

Kingston and I were just discussing whether I should expand. I argued against it, but if I work with out-of-town clients, perhaps a small shop will be necessary. "I don't have a storefront. Typically, I go to the client for measurements and fittings, and do the work from my home."

"I'm desperate." Had I not seen the atrocious modifications to his pants myself, I'd think Igor's frantic tone was dramatic. "It's only a matter of time before the fans notice. The team's social media crew takes photos and video of our arrivals at the rink and on the way to the plane for road trips. I've been lucky so far, but luck won't last forever."

Brock drops a toothpick from a bacon wrapped cantaloupe ball onto his plate. "Right? I never thought playing hockey would require so much thought about what I wear."

"Dude, I end up walking with my back to walls so they won't catch a glimpse." His massive shoulders shiver. "I look like I've just escaped the Gulag and am trying to avoid the searchlights and dogs."

The way he's looking at me with so much hope, I feel like a tailoring superhero. "I'll take your measurements this weekend, and later we can discuss your style, fabrics, and what you're looking for."

"If you can make me look as good as Leif and Calder, I'll fly to you. Or fly you out to me. Whatever it takes." Igor's young pup energy is on full display when he slaps me on the back with such force I nearly stumble into Brock.

After regaining my balance, I straighten my tie. "Text me your availability tomorrow, and I'll get you measured."

"Cool." Igor looks across the room and raises his hand at someone. "I've got to go. I brought my mom with me and I don't want her to think I ditched her."

Brock shifts his plate to his left hand and holds out his right hand. "Good luck tomorrow."

"You too." Igor takes Brock's hand, pulling him into a hug, and I have to hide my chuckle when Brock holds his plate out to the side to avoid wearing the fig pastry. Releasing Brock, Igor says, "I'll text you. Tell Calder I'll see him tomorrow."

The big man practically skips away, and this time I don't hold back my smile. He's going to be fun to work with.

"Can you take my measurements too?" Brock moves closer.

I take out my phone and set a reminder to follow up with him and Igor tomorrow. "Sure. Would you mind if I see you and Igor at the same time? I do that with Leif and Calder. It's more efficient."

"That's fine. I like Calder's stuff, but I can't pull off something like that." He looks down at his suit. "This isn't me either."

"Hey guys." Leif clasps my shoulder. "Where's Calder?"

I lift my chin in the direction Calder headed. "He's searching out food."

"Brock, have you met my partner, Jalen?" Leif wraps his arm around Jalen, pulling him into our group.

"Congratulations on a great season." The lighting of the room makes the purple tips of Jalen's hair a deeper hue, accenting his tie, and I wonder if his tie choice was purposeful.

I gesture to Leif's jacket. "Show Brock your lining."

Leif doesn't question my request, unbuttoning his double breasted light French beige jacket and holds it open to reveal the champagne colored lining decorated with drawings of stick people holding hands, stick dogs, rainbows, and an assortment of other scribbles. "My daughter Thea drew these last year when she was three."

"That's awesome." Brock leans in, getting a closer look. The corners of his mouth twitch and he points to a spiky yellow blob. "Is that Striker?"

Leif stands straighter, pride radiating from every inch of him. "Pretty good for a toddler, huh?"

"There are a lot of things we can do to make a garment yours. Everything from the cut, to the fabric, to the buttons can create a style that's you. Even something as simple as your socks or a pocket square can show your personality." I point to Jalen. "See how he's coordinated his pocket square with his socks?"

Jalen lifts his pant leg to reveal rainbow striped socks.

I scan Brock's outfit. The cognac shoes are a sophisticated version of a penny loafer and have a sleek silhouette. "Good choice on your loafers."

"Thanks?" Brock raises his left brow like he's unsure if I'm serious. "I like your jacket." Like he did with Calder, Brock rubs the fabric of my sleeve between his fingertips. "What is this?"

"Hey!" Calder wedges his body between Brock and me, shoving the plate of hors d'oeuvres at Leif, who, with the help of Jalen, catches it before everything topples to the floor. "Get your hands off him."

Brock jerks his hand back, then narrows his eyes at Calder. I'm familiar with such looks. They scream, I'm going to trifle with you, and enjoy it. "We were talking about his fabric."

"Yeah, well..." Calder's mouth gapes like he's not sure what to say. "Get your own tailor. He's mine." He grabs my arm and tugs. "Let's go."

I follow. There's a strange energy between Calder and Brock, so I wait until we're out of earshot to say, "I thought part of me being here was to drum up more business. Telling potential clients to get their own tailor defeats the purpose."

"He looked like he wanted you for more than tailoring." His gait is purposeful as he strides to the elevator, ignoring the people calling his name. He punches the *up* button once, twice, three times in rapid succession. "Fucking Brock. Always a pain in my ass."

The elevator doors open and I hold Calder back before he plows into an elderly couple exiting. Once inside, neither of us says anything. Waves of fury billow off him, and I feel like a chew toy being fought over by two dogs.

I close my eyes and inhale. This is why one should never agree to a weekend-long first date. I exhale. There is too much time for it to go sideways.

Once we're inside the room, I take a healthy swig of my drink. The burn down my throat overpowers the sweetness of the strawberries and feels apropos to the current situation.

Calder flops onto the bed, his arms spread wide as he stares at the ceiling. I should be mad, or at least irritated by his outburst, but his pained expression softens me. Knowing how hard he's worked this season and witnessing his nervousness earlier in the evening propels me to sit on the edge of the bed next to him.

"I'm sorry." He grasps my hand, bringing it to rest on his chest. "Since we were teens, I've let Brock bring out the worst in me. Tonight was no exception."

"What is it about him?" I keep my tone soft as the banging of his heart vibrates against my palm.

He closes his eyes, but strokes my hand. "I don't know. Our dads played in the league, and we hung out a lot as kids. Some events would get boring after a while, so Brock and I would make up games, hide from our parents... Stupid kids doing stupid kid stuff."

The air conditioner kicks on, a subtle hum in the otherwise quiet room. I want to know more, to understand what happened downstairs, but I remain silent, giving Calder time.

"I thought we were friends." He opens his eyes, and the dejection in them traps me in my spot. "When I was sixteen, both our dads were playing in an alumni game during All-Star weekend. Brock and I had gone in the past and always had fun together. But that year, he was different, acting like he was better than me, saying shitty stuff, and avoiding me. After that, every time I saw him, it was the same. When our teams played each other in the championship during our junior year of college, my team won. I was MVP, and Brock seemed like he hated me. We didn't exchange a single word sitting in the same room at the draft." He slings his free arm over his eyes, but continues to hold my hand to his chest. "To this day, I don't get what happened. In the beginning, I tried asking him if I did something, but he'd blow me off."

The rhythm of his heart thumping against my palm slows, finally steadying. "He hurt your feelings."

He rolls to his side, cupping my hand between his two bigger ones, and tucks them under his chin. "I'm a professional hockey player. My feelings don't get hurt."

I lay down, facing him. "I forgot professional athletes are immune to hurt feelings."

Other than working with Leif and a few others from the Power, my experience with jocks was in high school. And I would not classify those experiences as positive. My people are creatives, nerds, and the like, and that's who I've dated. From our first meeting, Calder seemed different, and witnessing his vulnerability reinforces my initial assessment.

"We are. It's in our contracts." He inches closer, the crease in the middle of his bottom lip pulling taut.

I scoot closer too, eliminating the scant space between us. "Is that under the 'no crying in baseball' clause?"

"How'd you know?" The tip of his nose brushes my earlobe and his breath heats my neck before his tongue wets my skin. "I'm sorry for acting like a jealous asshole."

I wind my leg over his, securing him. "If you're truly apologetic, you'd show me."

"Yeah?" He tugs my lobe between his teeth. "What'd you have in mind?"

Trailing my fingers down his front, I unbutton his jacket and pull his dress shirt from his trousers. Heat radiates from every inch of him and feeling his skin seems as necessary as breathing. "What I have in mind requires disrobing in order to keep your jacket in pristine condition."

"I love when you talk clothing. What else have you got for me?" He kisses the tip of my nose.

I snake my palm under his shirt, absorbing all of that delicious heat, and loving the quiver of his stomach under my touch. "Garment-washed."

"Oh, baby, tell me more." Even with his light-hearted banter, his voice is like a purr that sends my need into overdrive.

I lower my voice as I explore the muscled abdomen I can't wait to see. "Inseam, scye, overweaving–"

"Not overweaving," he moans and palms my bottom. "I may come in my pants with overweaving."

Laughing, I push him. "Would naming fabrics be better for you?"

"Hell, no. You mention merino wool, and I won't be held responsible for ripping off your clothes." Another kiss on the nose and he bolts to sitting, shucking out of his jacket. "Give me yours and I'll hang them. I don't want you worrying about creases."

I stand to remove my jacket, hand it to him, and place my hand over my heart like I'm an actor in one of Kingston's productions as Calder heads toward the closet. "Foreplay at its finest."

The rumble of laughter fills the room, wrapping around me like a suit made from Donegal tweed wool, warm and soft and sleek.

In seconds, he's stalking back, unbuttoning his shirt sleeves. His blond hair tousled, eyes as dark as the midnight sky, and muscled form flexing with every step, he looks like a lion ready to pounce. My throat bobs at the sight.

"You're gorgeous," I say.

Nimble fingers work the buttons of the front of his shirt until the white cotton hangs open, revealing a broad chest, his fair skin tight and toned. He slips the shirt from his shoulders, letting it drop to the floor. "I want to see you."

"Yes." The word is a rasp. I trail a finger over the pale blue vein that runs from the top of his right pec to his biceps and down his forearm.

He watches my finger until it reaches the end. Grasping my wrist, he keeps his gaze locked on me as he brings the finger to his mouth and sucks it. My knees weaken and I clutch the waist of his pants for purchase. The corner of his mouth ticks up. A swirl of his tongue and he releases my finger.

"What do you say to losing this?" He tugs on my shirt. "And these?" A tug of my pants.

"Merino wool."

His head falls back with the boom of his laughter, and when his eyes meet mine again, I'm buoyed by the intensity of affection I see in them. "You undo the shirt. I've got your pants." Before I can process what he's said, my pants and underwear are at my ankles and Calder is on his knees, his hands gripping my bottom, and his hot breath whispering over the base of my stomach. "Shirt, Riggs."

As quickly as my fingers will go, which is not fast enough, I loosen my buttons and toss the shirt to the chair. Calder's mouth is everywhere. My hip bone, my waist, the inside of my thigh. The faintest swipe of his tongue along my balls spurs a whimper from my throat. Hands everywhere, mouth everywhere, but not where I need them.

"More." I rock my hips forward. "I need more."

"Mmmm." He drags his tongue up my cock and white spots prick at my vision. "I need more too." Circling the tip of my weeping slit, he flicks his tongue, lapping me up.

My head drops forward. The view of him taking me into his mouth is almost as scorching as the wet heat consuming me. But I want more. "Not like this."

Instantly, he releases me, his eyes glazed and a little wild. "You don't want to?"

"I want to." I pull him to his feet, kissing him hard. "Lose the pants and get on the bed." Thankful I chose loafers tonight, I toe them off, step out of my puddled pants, and rip off my socks.

Calder dives onto the bed, his naked body on full display. Part of me wants to take a moment to appreciate his magnificent form, but I've spent months admiring him from afar, evaluating him with a professional eye. With the opportunity to touch him the way I've only dreamed about, I have no intention of wasting a second.

I crawl over him, straddling his face and licking my lips as I dip my head and take his length into my mouth. My insides vibrate with his moan. Powerful hands grip my hips and tug me, not so gently, to him. I nearly explode when he swallows my hardness. Grinding my hips into his face as he works my shaft, drawing it in deeper and deeper.

His hips jerk and I relax my jaw to take more of him. He's thick and hot and better than anything I could have imagined. Insatiable for him, I inhale his citrus scent mixed with the musk of arousal, wishing I could bottle it. I grip the base of his cock, jacking in time with his thrusts. Palms smooth over my thighs and bottom, and then a finger finds my hole.

"Yes." His cock pops from my mouth and I push into him as I keep pumping. "So good." My head drops and my teeth find the inside of his thigh. He jerks and sucks in his cheeks, creating the most intoxicating pressure. "Fuck."

I can feel him smile around my dick before he releases me. "I've never heard you swear before."

"You've never blown me before." I peer at him over my shoulder, his lips swollen and glistening and the smuggest expression ever.

His chuckle eggs me on to make him swear too. With a flick of my tongue, I lap his precum, then take him. Opening my throat, I swallow him until I'm nose deep in his balls.

"Shit, Riggs. Fuck." His hips pump and he consumes me.

Unhindered hunger devours us. My cock pulses, and my heart races, swooshing in my ears. Saliva dribbles down my chin, and I gag from the power of Calder's thrusts. But my appetite for him is all-consuming. The sensation of cool sheets under my knees, the slick skin under my torso, and the soft scrape of his whiskers against the inside of my thigh are all heightened by this thirst, this craving.

A frisson of pleasure sprints up my spine, and my balls contract before my orgasm erupts, bursting from me like a lightning strike hitting a transformer. Sparks fly, lighting up the night as my muscles spasm, and I lose control over my movements until he groans and tangy cream hits the back of my throat. Wanting everything he has, I drink him down, savoring the salty sweetness, even as flashes behind my eyes fire bright with every twirl of his tongue and kiss of his lips.

When he finally releases me, I collapse onto him, my cheek resting below his knee. Air heaves in and out of my chest, and soft kisses press to my calf. I release a long, satisfied sigh. "That was lovely."

"Come up here." His voice is rough and sexy, and he taps my ankle.

I roll off him and crawl up the bed. He lifts his bottom, tugging the sheets down, then holds them open for me to slip under. Once we're both tucked in, he pulls me to him and I nestle into his side.

He skims a finger up and down my arm, the movement hypnotic. "I would happily give up the Rookie of the Year nomination to do that again."

"Lucky for you, you don't have to." I tweak his rosy nipple.

”I *am* lucky.“ He kisses the top of my head.

I drag my fingertips over his torso in lazy figure-eights, sated and heart full. "I am too."

Chapter Three

♥

Calder

I WAKE TO A warm body pressed against my side and Riggs' arm across my chest. His head is on my shoulder and his breath flutters over my skin. I'm pleasantly surprised he's a cuddler like me. That we sought each other out in sleep makes me smile, and hope there will be more to our relationship than this one weekend.

He gives a sleepy sigh and nuzzles into my neck, his soft hair tickling my chin. Pressing a kiss to his crown is an automatic gesture that catches me once my lips are in contact with the soft brown tresses. Why does being affectionate with him so quickly feel so natural?

Riggs stretches, arching his back, and blinks open his eyes. In the muted morning light, the hazel reminds me of jade. He brushes his lips over my cheek. "Morning."

"It is a good morning." I give into the urge to stroke my hand over the muscles in his back. I like the way we fit together. "Sleep well?"

"I did." Rubbing his calf over mine, he cuddles in closer. "So, what's the plan for today? You mentioned an interview?"

"I have one at ten o'clock with Harley Stone for his podcast. Then nothing else until the awards show." On the bedside table, my phone beeps. I grab it and find a message from Harley.

Harley: Hey Calder, I met Igor and Brock in the hotel bar last night and invited them to join us for the interview. I'll have coffee and breakfast waiting.

Riggs raises a brow at my stiffening shoulders. I angle the phone so he can see the text and fight against irritation rising like spikes. "I'm getting company at the interview."

Sympathy creases his features. His muscles flex against mine as he reaches for his phone. "I know being around Brock isn't easy for you. Perhaps my being there could help? I'll text him and Igor and see if I can take their measurements then."

Something in my chest warms at his offer to soothe the situation and how easy he made it. I lift my arm, welcoming him back to my side. "I'd like that. It would be convenient too. Then we'd have the rest of the day free."

His fingers fly over the keypad. "Have you met Harley before?"

"I was a guest on his podcast twice this season. He's Ryder's brother, so he also hangs out with us sometimes. Their brother Grayson is Thea's manny."

"Grayson was at Leif's when I did a fitting for him last year." Riggs' phone chimes. He swipes his thumb across the screen. "Brock and Igor are fine with doing the measurements then. We don't have much time. Why don't you shower while I figure out what I'm wearing?"

I marvel at the way the light plays over his skin as he rises from the bed. "Do you always wear suits to fittings?"

"I like to look professional." He pauses at the closet. "Though, if we're heading out afterward, I don't want to be overdressed."

The sheet shifted to my waist when he rolled out of bed. I push away the soft material and swing my legs over the side of the mattress. The chill of the air-conditioning raises goosebumps. "Plus, it's like ninety degrees outside. I don't want you getting heat stroke. Though I'd totally take care of you if you did. Wear whatever you want. We can always stop back here so you can change clothes before we head out."

His smile is almost shy. "You won't mind stopping back here?"

"Of course not." I wonder if someone else wasn't as accommodating. I don't know how anyone could deny him anything. "I'll sit through as many costume changes as you want."

That gets me a smile rivaling the sun's brightness. A glance at the clock reminds me we're running out of time, so I hurry into the bathroom to shower and brush my teeth.

When I step out, with a towel wrapped around my waist, Riggs' appreciative perusal of my body makes me throb. Clothes in hand, he brushes past me, his fingertips grazing my side, spiking heat through my system. The bathroom door closes, the shower turns on, and I rifle through my clothes. If I were here alone, I'd stroll up to Harley's suite in shorts and a t-shirt. But I don't want Riggs to feel I'm too underdressed, so I choose khaki shorts and a short sleeve button-down that he made for me. Its orange and pink pattern reminds me of sunsets.

The bathroom door opens. Steam billows out like a smoke machine, preceding Riggs' entrance. My mouth goes dry and I nearly swallow my tongue. In his tan suit and light blue shirt, he could be a runway model. "You look amazing."

There's that shy smile again. "Thank you. I love that shirt on you."

"I have a great tailor." I take hold of his hand. It curls securely around mine. I'm tempted to say something about our hands being a perfect fit, but don't know if he'd think I'm pushing too hard, too fast, so I settle for raising them to my lips and pressing a kiss to his knuckles. "You ready to go?"

His gaze is soft, holding mine, and he nods. "I need my phone and that small kit on the desk."

I pocket the keycard and my phone, then follow him into the hall. He stays close to my side during the long walk down the hallway and the elevator ride up ten floors.

Outside Harley's suite, I pause and draw in a deep breath. Riggs lays his hand on the center of my back. "You have this. And, I'm here."

"Thank you." I lean in for a kiss. With his mouth soft and pliant under mine, the quick brush of lips to show my gratitude lingers and lengthens. He winds his arms around me. My heart opens wider, like it's been waiting for him.

With a click and a creak, the door swings open. "Well, this is a nice sight." Harley's warm voice draws our attention.

I raise my head and turn toward the man. "Hey, Harley. How're you doing?"

He grins. "Not as well as you. Come in, the others are here."

"Ryder, Leif, and Sawyer?" I can only hope.

"Nope. I'm interviewing them later. Brock and Igor." He beckons us to enter, then shakes hands with Riggs. "Riggs, Igor told me you were joining us. Nice to meet you."

"You as well." Riggs holds up the kit. "I hope you don't mind. The measurements won't take long."

"Neither will the interview." Harley leads the way into the suite. "Actually, since you're dressing some of the Power players, I'd love to have you join in the interview and talk more about that. Give our listeners an inside look."

Riggs' eyes widen and his mouth works open, then closed before curving into a smile. "I'd enjoy that very much."

I'm thrilled for him. Harley's audience is huge. This could lead to more clients for Riggs.

In an area with two small couches and a table laden with breakfast foods, Igor and Brock sit side by side, though Brock is slumped forward, cradling his head in his hands. There's a large coffee and an orange juice in front of him. Igor stands and gives me a hug, murmuring, "Brock is hungover."

Wincing, he raises his head and reaches for the juice. "Hello."

Harley gestures at his computer and the microphones set up on another table in a secluded nook at the opposite end of the suite. "While Brock gets more fluids and some food into him, I'll interview Calder and Igor. Then, we'll bring in Riggs. I'll save Brock for last, and can edit in his answers so it sounds like he's chatting with us. Brock, are you sure you don't want to do your interview another day? It's not a problem."

Brock lowers his juice and shoots us an apologetic look. "I'll be fine. Just don't shout."

"No one is shouting." The shields I've learned to raise whenever I'm around Brock stay down. My whole life, he was the one person who knew exactly what I was going through, because he was going through the same. This year, I felt his absence from my life more keenly than the last few.

After giving my shoulder a squeeze, Riggs glides toward Brock. "We can do your measurements another time."

"No, we can do them now. I don't want to put you out." With a wince, Brock pushes to his feet.

Riggs nods and opens the kit holding his tape measure and a tablet that stores whatever program or app he uses to record client information.

I follow Igor and Harley to the podcast table, and we get started. As we chat, my attention stays half-focused on the pair across the room. Brock looks sad, like he hasn't a friend in the world. He keeps glancing at me as Riggs takes measurements and makes notes.

"Calder," Harley's voice jolts me. "How is it being in the same room with Brock after what went down during round one in the playoffs?"

Axel's words of warning echo in my thoughts. "Awkward. Us players have long memories and that round wasn't that long ago. You attempt to take out my captain's knees again, Zagras, and we won't be exchanging any niceties."

Regret flickers across Brock's features. He wanders to the table and sits beside me. "What I did was a dick move. Being frustrated is no excuse."

"Nope." I take a sip of water. "Some argue that my taking revenge wasn't a smart move either. I disagree. And, yes, Axel, if you're listening, I know I shouldn't be saying that."

Harley and Igor chuckle, and Harley makes a notation on the pad in front of him. "I'm definitely playing this for Axel when I interview him later."

Since Brock is sitting here, Harley asks him the same questions he asked Igor and me earlier, then he beckons Riggs to us. "Riggs, I want to ask you about how you got started designing suits and how you work with your sports clients, then walk us through the measurements you take for a bespoke suit, using Igor. Brock and Calder, you're done. Go eat."

"Before I go," I lean into the mic. "I want to give my endorsement of Riggs."

Harley hits a key on the keyboard to continue recording and motions for me to go ahead. "I'll edit it so the flow works."

"Riggs is the best tailor. He really listens to what a client is looking for and always exceeds my expectations. You can trust he'll take good care of you." The weight of Riggs' hand is warm on my shoulder. I look up at him and smile. "There's no one else for me, only Riggs."

"Nice job, Calder." Harley presses another key to pause the recording.

I stand and Riggs frames my face with his hands. Eyes sparkling, he kisses me.

Aware of our audience, I gesture for him to claim my chair, then follow Brock to the opposite end of the suite.

He claims his coffee with a grateful groan. After taking a deep drink, he glances at me and rubs his hand over his chin. "When you punched me, I was afraid you'd broken my jaw."

"You got good hits too." I pour myself a coffee. "I had bruises for over a week."

His bloodshot eyes fill with remorse. "I'm sorry. About everything."

The others are occupied with the interview, and I don't know if I'll ever get another chance to talk to Brock like this, and discover what went wrong. "What's your deal? Why do you hate me?"

"Nothing I do is good enough." Moving gingerly, he lowers himself onto the couch. "My dad is constantly on me about how I'm not you."

"What?" Keeping my voice to a whisper, I sit beside him.

"I heard it all the time, growing up. *Be more like Calder. Why aren't you more like Calder?* He put you on a freaking pedestal and no matter what I accomplished, I never measured up. After hearing that so many times, I resented you. More accurately, that I wasn't you, and I let it ruin our friendship."

I'm stunned... But also not. I knew enough players growing up whose parents' over-involvement ruined the game for them. I drop onto the cushion beside him. "Damn, Brock. I... I don't know what to say."

"Even my being selected first in the draft didn't help. This season, the pressure and criticism from him was nonstop, and everyone else comparing us made that echo chamber louder." With a wince, he drags his hand through his hair. "I had a breakdown after your team eliminated mine from the playoffs. That night, after the last game, it... wasn't a good time. I couldn't breathe, was having chest pains. Thought it was a heart attack. I went to the ER."

"Shit. Are you okay?"

He nods. "Turns out it was a panic attack. I was in a bad place. I started working with a sports psychologist a few weeks ago. It was that, or quit playing hockey."

I'm still reeling from the panic attack news, that he considered quitting hockey completely floors me. How bad things must have been to drive him to that point is heartbreaking. "I'm sorry. I wish I'd known."

The left corner of his mouth lifts in a half smile. "I don't know what you could've done. Besides switching parents with me."

"Dude." An ache throbs in my chest. Hesitant that he'll accept comfort from me, I lay my hand on his shoulder. He looks lost and lonely, and I wonder how much he's isolated himself from letting anyone in.

Eyeing my hand on his shoulder, he smiles and leans in, resting against my side for a moment. "I have a long way to go, but I'm in a better place. Winning tonight would make my dad happy."

For the first time since I got the nomination, I don't want to win. Brock needs that trophy. "Then I hope you do."

"Seriously?"

"Yeah. Look, my dad's great. I'm lucky. Yours..."

"Needs to find something to do other than play golf and nitpick me." Voice soft, he shifts his gaze to the wide window. "My psychologist and I are working on setting boundaries for my dad with the upcoming season, but I'm worried they won't be respected."

"Then you call me. I'm serious. Call me." His phone is hanging half off the edge of the table. I grab it and enter my contact info.

He blinks several times, his gaze glued on my face. "Really? After everything? What I said? How I acted?"

Renewing our friendship feels like a real possibility. I set his phone beside his coffee. "Look, I don't know how I would've behaved if I were in your shoes. I might've done the same thing. So let's put it behind us. I'm willing, if you are. I miss my friend."

Brock hugs me tight. "I do too. Thanks, man."

The embrace catches me off guard, but I quickly wrap my arms around him, happiness and hope overwhelming me, and hold on. When his grasp loosens, I lower my arms and am relieved to see his shaky smile growing stronger. "Looking better already."

"I'm feeling that way. Tomorrow, I'm escaping to the Caribbean for a week."

I realize I didn't see him with anyone last night at the reception. "You here alone?"

"Yeah." He shrugs like it's not a big deal, but his tight shoulders suggest otherwise.

"Sit with us tonight."

He blinks in surprise. "You have a full table already with your teammates and their guests."

"We'll manage." I sip my coffee. Harley, Igor, and Riggs are heading toward us.

Igor plucks a piece of melon from a fruit bowl. "Brock can sit with me. My teammate isn't coming. His wife went into labor."

Harley grabs a plate, then gestures for us to do the same. "I'll see you at the show too. Axel gave me his extra ticket."

With Brock on one side of me and Riggs on the other, I dig into my breakfast. The conversation is lighthearted with talk of suit ideas for Brock and Igor.

After all the food has been devoured, we bid goodbye to the guys and Riggs and I slip into the hallway. He links our hands together. "I didn't hear all of what was said, but I caught enough. Poor guy. I'm glad you were able to clear the air."

"Me too." Thinking about Brock, my heart is heavy. "What do you want to do now? The city and all that's in it is open to you."

"The exhibit we saw yesterday was for me. So let's do something you'd like."

I hit the button for the elevator and draw him against my side. "Honestly? I just want to spend time with you."

"You're guaranteed to get that, but you still need to pick an activity."

"Can we visit Central Park? Maybe see the animals at the zoo? I need funny antics to take my mind off the number Brock's dad did on him."

Riggs leads me into the elevator. "Operation cheer up Calder is about to commence. Let's pop down to our room so I can change clothes. A three-piece suit is a bit formal for the zoo."

I run a fingertip along the V of his vest. "I don't know about that. The penguins look like they're wearing tuxedos."

Laughing, Riggs pulls me in for a kiss. "I knew I liked you."

"Yeah? I like you too."

·♥·♥·♥·♥·♥·

Drained from long hours out in the sun, I push open the door to our hotel room and hold it so Riggs can enter first. He whips off his sweat-drenched shirt and heads for the small refrigerator, then tosses me a bottle of water before downing the contents of another.

I'm entranced, watching his throat work and the slickness of his muscles. He lifts a brow. "You going to drink yours?"

"Uh, yeah. As soon as I recover from the gorgeous sight you make." I twist off the bottle cap. Cold water hits my lips. The first gulp, and nothing has ever tasted so good. I upend the bottle, draining it.

Riggs' hungry gaze drinks me in. "Talk about a gorgeous sight."

I glance at my soaked shirt. "What me?"

"Yes, you." Graceful steps eliminate the space separating us. "Thank you for a fun afternoon."

"I kept you outside for hours in ninety degree heat."

He trails a fingertip down my chest. "We had a charming stroll through a park, saw a castle and a zoo, and went on a romantic horse-drawn carriage ride. Plus iced coffee and gelato and a lovely meal at an outdoor café."

I suck in a breath as his hand lingers on the button closest to the hem. "You really liked it?"

"Calder, I don't have a good poker face. If I didn't like it, you'd be able to tell." Nimble fingers work the button free, then rise to tackle the next.

I start at my top button, stealing a kiss for each one we free. Our hands meet at the middle of my torso and I catch his in my grasp. "Share a shower with me?"

"You read my mind." He nips my lower lip. I rip my shirt off, desperate for the feel of skin on skin. His torso is warm against mine and sweat intensifies his scent. It's all so good, I wish I could bottle up this moment.

We separate to free ourselves of our shorts, boxers, and shoes. A naked Riggs is a tempting sight. Every cell throbs with the need to touch and devour. He links our hands together and draws me to the bathroom. In between kisses, I get the shower started. He follows me under the spray and we reach for each other, the movement automatic, as natural as if we've been sharing showers for months.

Heat, steam, the slide of wet skin, our hands roaming, lips meeting again and again, the sensations layer over each other, immersing me in a hurricane that is Riggs.

His cock is as hard as mine, rubbing against my hip. I grab a handful of conditioner, then wrap my hand around us. We both groan and he takes our kiss deeper, tangling our tongues as I jack us together.

The slick slide of his cock against mine is as intoxicating as his kisses. Riggs' eyes are misty with desire. His hand joins mine, tightening our grip, and the teasing twist he adds to the top of the strokes pushes me hard and fast to the edge.

His other hand digs into my shoulder like he can't hold me tight enough, and he pumps his hips into mine. "So good, Calder. I'm nearly there."

"Me too." I hate having to rush, but we need to be downstairs soon. I want to take my time with him, a lazy and thorough exploration where we learn each other's secrets.

I move my other hand from bracing against the wall behind Riggs' head and clamp it to his hip. Holding tight, I drive into him, chasing the pleasure building higher and higher. With a moan, Riggs slams his mouth against mine. His release pulses over our hands.

Another thrust, and I'm there, spiraling into a million pieces, painting his stomach, my knees going weak, and my head thrown back. His hands hold strong, supporting me. Soft kisses trail over my throat as my senses come back online. I lift my head and catch Riggs' satisfied smile.

Our kisses are lazy and indulgent. He trails his hands along my sides before handing me the soap. I rub it over myself, watching him work shampoo into his hair. He really is gorgeous.

Catching my stare, he smiles again before sticking his head under the spray. We switch places and products, and I love the way his eyes trail over me as I rush to shampoo and rinse.

I hand him a towel before grabbing another for myself. We dress, accompanied by music from Riggs' phone.

After giving myself a once-over in the mirror, I turn to Riggs. His gray linen suit has hints of teal in it and his shirt matches my suit shade. I hold out my hand for him. "We're coordinated."

"Is that okay?" Dragging his teeth over his lower lip, he smooths a hand over his herringbone patterned tie.

"More than okay." I gather him into my arms and kiss him. "In fact, it's perfect."

·♥·♥·♥·♥·♥·

Walking into the hotel's ballroom with Riggs's hand linked with mine, I ride the wave of nerves. The tingling is fainter than the rush of anticipation I get before games, but still there, circulating, making everything seem *more*. Or maybe that's simply because of the man at my side.

The room is filled with the game's greatest players. Being here among them, as a nominee, is surreal. Understanding why Igor was awestruck by Leif is easy. I feel the same way about a few of the veteran players. Sometimes, I still can't believe they're my peers.

I need to make up for cutting our time with the other players short at last night's reception, so we make the rounds and I introduce Riggs to everyone we meet. He hands out a lot of business cards.

Leif, Jalen, Sawyer, Axel, Harley, and Ryder are already seated at our table. I hug the guys then slide into a seat between Leif and Riggs. "What are we talking about?"

Leif leans his forearm on my shoulder. "The podcast interviews. Harley played a portion of yours for us."

"He did?" I laugh, then look at Axel. "Sorry, but I couldn't help myself."

He gives me a wry smile. "I'm sure."

Harley sips his drink. "I got Axel's reaction recorded too. Podcast gold. Wait till you hear it. I'm combining all the interviews into one show."

Riggs' hand on my thigh pulls my attention. He nods at the table behind us. "Brock and Igor are here."

We exchange waves. I'm relieved Brock's color looks better, though nerves pull his features taut.

Waitstaff circulate with drinks and trays of desserts. We chat about how everyone spent their day, then the lights dim, and the emcee takes the stage and gets the show underway.

Leif heads up to present the first award of the night, for the most defensive forward. We watch video highlights of the nominees on a screen that runs the length of the stage, and the weight of the ceremony hits me. Things I did this season were good enough to get me here, as a part of hockey history, just a small blip, but a blip nonetheless. That I get to share it with my friends and Riggs makes it mean so much more.

Award after award, I chat and cheer, drinking champagne and sharing bites of desserts with Riggs.

Axel presents his award, followed by the presenter announcing the outstanding defenseman award. Leif's highlights fill the screen, and I cross my fingers, willing him to win.

"And the award goes to Leif Larsson."

Our table erupts in cheers. Leif seems stunned. He kisses Jalen, hugs me and the others, then strides to the stage. Our celebration grows louder as he accepts the trophy and again as he thanks us in his speech.

Sawyer doesn't win the community award, but he lifts his glass in toast to the winner and Harley promises to host a live podcast recording at a pet adoption event, earning a smile from our favorite goalie and assurances we'll all be involved in the event.

The emcee is back. "Our final award tonight is the Rookie of the Year award. It recognizes the best first-year player in the league. Let's take a look at the nominees."

Highlights of Brock's season fill the screen, then a graphic with his stats, sixty-one points, twenty-three goals, and thirty-eight assists. Then my highlights begin and Riggs squeezes my hand. My stats appear, twenty-three goals, forty assists, my sixty-three points leading all rookies. Leif claps me on the back and my friends lift their glasses in toast. Igor's highlights finish off the video. His stats are impressive too. Fifty points, which led all rookie defensemen, forty-three assists, and he led all rookies in ice time and minutes-per-game.

"And the award goes to Igor Vasilevski."

The room bursts into applause. I let out a piercing whistle and Igor grins at me.

He ascends the stage, takes hold of the trophy, thanks his teammates and family, then he looks at Brock and me. "I'd like to thank my fellow nominees, Brock and Calder. I met them this weekend as strangers, but we're leaving as friends."

Damn right we are. I nod at him, then Brock.

The emcee is back, thanking everyone for attending tonight. The lights brighten, and the room fills with chatter.

I tap Riggs' hand. "Let's congratulate Igor. I want to check on Brock too."

"Sure."

We head over and Igor gives us an exuberant hug. More players join us. Igor introduces Riggs to a potential client. Tugging on Brock's sleeve, I pull him aside. "You doing okay?"

He shrugs, then nods. "I'm glad I can put this season to rest."

"When you get back from your vacation, text me. We can train together. Be friends. Support each other."

Smile wobbling, Brock pulls me into a tight hug. "Friends. I like that, a lot. I'll text you."

"You better." I return the fierce embrace, imbuing all the hope I have into it.

We separate. More people swarm in, and Brock is drawn into a conversation with Igor's mom.

Riggs slips his arm through mine, studying me with an expression so sweet, my heart aches and yearns. "I'm sorry you didn't win."

In a room filled with big stars and gleaming trophies, he outshines them all. He both settles me and makes me soar, an odd combination I've never felt before. "I have you here with me, so I feel like I've won."

Smiling, he lays his hand over my heart. "Does this mean you want to keep seeing me after this weekend?"

"I do." I cup his face in my hand, soaking up his scent and the feel of his body along mine. Anticipation thrums through me, heady and potent. "This is the start of something amazing."

"I agree." Riggs presses his lips to mine, a promise wrapped in sweetness and heat.

I may not have won Rookie of the Year, but for Riggs, I'll always strive to be the world's best boyfriend.

Chapter Four

♥

Riggs

"Hold still or I'll prick you." I remove a straight pin from the pin cushion strapped to my wrist and pin the side seam of Calder's burgundy silk trousers. "And this fabric is too gorgeous to have bloodstains."

Fingertips continue to twirl in my hair, but at least he's still on the stepstool in the makeshift fitting area we've created in the middle of his living room. "Who are you kidding? You could pin a suit on a moving target, eyes closed, without a prick."

"If you can work with Sawyer without drawing blood, there's nothing you can't do, Riggs." Feet propped on an ottoman and arms spread open along the back of the couch, Axel smiles. His image reflects to me through the portable mirror that now lives at Calder's place.

Behind the couch, kicking a yellow Striker hacky sack, Sawyer plucks the back of Axel's head while keeping the hacky sack in play. "Hey. I'm a great customer."

"Better than this one." I rise from my crouched position and circle Calder, inspecting my work. "Just a few nips here and there, and it'll be perfect for the season opener."

It's been almost three months since our weekend-long first date. Between the increase in orders that came in because of the players I met and Harley's podcast, and most of my free time spent with Calder, the summer was a whirlwind. Things don't look like they'll slow down with the hockey season beginning in less than two weeks.

I take a final look at Calder in the mirror and smooth my palm over the perfection that is his backside, giving it a pat. His lapis gaze captures me and he blows a kiss at my reflection. "You're done. Be careful when you take them off."

"You could help me." The exaggerated wiggle of his brows is paired with an equally exaggerated wink.

I bite my bottom lip, but it does little to withhold the laughter that bubbles from my chest. There's no concealing my joy when he's near.

"No fooling around until Riggs is done with my fitting," Sawyer says.

"And we're out of here." Axel twists the cap from his water bottle and takes a swig. "There are certain things I don't want to know about my tailor *or* MacKinnon."

Sawyer sticks out his bottom lip in an exaggerated pout. "Axel feels left out with PDAs when he can't have Harley."

"I do not." A flush creeps up Axel's cheeks and he throws a pillow at Sawyer, who expertly stops the flying object in mid-air, his enormous hand easily catching it. "My relationship with Harley is professional, just as his is with you two."

Sawyer tosses the hacky sack to Calder and they share a look. "Go change so I can try on my suits."

"You should have changed while Riggs was pinning his pants." Scowling at his water bottle, Axel looks more like Thea when she feels she's been treated unfairly than the captain of a professional hockey team. Were he not so formidable on the ice and would probably not appreciate my characterization, I'd say his reaction was adorable.

Calder's soft lips press to mine. "Back in a minute."

In the months since Calder and I started dating, I've become accustomed to the flutter in my chest whenever he's present. Or when I receive a text from him... Or think about him. I can't help my grin as I watch him toss the hacky sack at Sawyer, bonking him in the head.

"Hey!" Sawyer launches the pillow at Calder, missing him as Calder jogs to his bedroom, his laughter trailing behind.

Axel shakes his head, but his mouth twitches with amusement as he meets my gaze. "They're like children."

Sawyer points to the empty hallway. "He started it."

"You make my point." Axel drops his feet to the floor, resting his elbows on his knees. "Can you make jeans, Riggs?"

I jot down some notes for Calder's suit. "Suits are my specialty, but working with denim is no problem."

"Because I hate shopping for jeans. By the time I have you alter them, I'm spending a small fortune. I'd rather pay you and have exactly what I want."

Donning gray athletic pants that hug his thighs in the most delicious way, Calder rejoins us. "My man can make anything."

I open a new tab in my notes app. "What do you want that you're not getting now?"

"Movement," Sawyer says. "Even the jeans that are supposed to have spandex in them feel stiff. I want to move like I do in sweats."

"That." Axel nods at Sawyer and catches the pillow Calder tosses to him, then places it on the couch. "I also want more variety."

"Such as?" I ask as I jot notes.

The plastic crinkles as Axel squeezes the empty water bottle. "Jeans for working around the house. Dressier jeans for dates—"

"When have you gone on a date recently?" Sawyer bumps Axel's foot with his.

Axel narrows his eyes at the grinning Sawyer. "Shouldn't you be changing?"

Sawyer waves away Axel's words and plops down next to his captain. "This is more interesting."

"So something with a looser fit for your grunt work, and more fitted, maybe in a dark wash for going out?" Ideas come faster than I can type and my hand aches to create. I reach for my sketch pad and flip to a blank page.

"I get what you're saying, Axel." Calder props his bottom on the arm of the chair I've commandeered, and I lean into his warmth. "There's something about the custom fit that makes it hard to go back to buying off the rack."

Sawyer removes the bottle from Axel's grip and the crinkling stops. "It's too bad not everyone has access to Riggs."

"Or can afford custom clothing." Axel leans into the cushions. "Look at those college guys. Most of them live in athletic wear because that's the only thing that fits. That's what I did."

"Me too," says Sawyer.

"Same," says Calder.

Axel folds brawny arms that make finding properly fitting shirts difficult over his expansive chest. "There's no way young guys can afford to have a pair of jeans tailored, let alone custom made. And it's hard to tell what jeans really look like or how comfortable they'll be before they're tailored."

My pencil scratches across the paper and I can feel Calder leaning closer to look over my shoulder. "You should start your own line."

"Yes!" Sawyer jumps up and pumps his arm in the air. "I would totally buy that."

I halt my sketching and look up to find the three of them staring at me. Sawyer's face is split in two, his head bobbing. Axel's expression is one of more consideration, but he, too, is nodding. And Calder beams at me, like he believes I can do anything. "I don't know anything about creating a line."

"Says the man who started a thriving business from his social media account." Calder wraps his arm over my shoulders, pulling me into a reassuring half hug.

Fingers drumming on his beefy biceps, Axel seems to consider his words. "I'm not an expert, but I think there's a market. Not only for professional players, but for college and high school. And not just hockey players, but for guys who are bigger. Look at Jalen. I'll bet he'd have a hard time finding clothes that fit even if he didn't play hockey."

"And we could help promote it." Sawyer's face is alight with excitement, as if having my own clothing line is a done deal.

It's not a terrible idea. Since seeing Igor's atrocious tailoring disasters, I've posted a few videos geared to men with hockey player builds on what to look for when purchasing clothing and when hiring a tailor. "I don't know... There's a lot to research and learn..."

"You could do it, easy." Calder presses a kiss to the top of my head. "Sawyer's right. We'd help you in any way we could." His belief in me is snuggling in a cashmere blanket in front of a fire on a cold winter day.

With their support, the thought of taking on a new venture doesn't seem so daunting. It may even be fun. "I guess there's no harm in doing some preliminary research. See if there's a market out there." I hand my sketch pad to Axel. "Here are some rough ideas that popped up while you were talking."

Axel studies the drawings, elbowing Sawyer, who keeps sticking his head over Axel's shoulder to see. "I can't believe you came up with these within minutes."

Sawyer points to the pad. "I like the third one. They'd be great for Saturday afternoon beer with the guys."

"You sound like an ad campaign." Calder rubs my arm.

As much as I'd like to stay snuggled into his side, I want to finish Sawyer's fittings because Calder and I have big plans to order from the Indian restaurant down the street and watch the final episode of the reality design show I got him hooked on. Tonight, we'll see the three finalists' runway collections and who will be crowned the best designer. I pry myself from my man and retrieve my sketches from Axel and Sawyer. "We can talk about these more later. Sawyer, go change. I have plans after we're done here."

"I thought we were ordering takeout and watching our show." Eyes wide, Calder stiffens on his perch.

I return my pad to my handmade vintage leather messenger bag next to the chair, squeezing Calder's knee as I straighten. "I was talking about our plans."

"I bet you could get Malcolm to be in an ad campaign," Sawyer calls as he heads down the hall to Calder's bedroom. "He's always posing like he thinks he's a model."

Axel points his chin to Sawyer's retreating back. "He's not wrong. Last season, I was trapped in a twenty-minute conversation with Malcolm about the best lighting for selfies after he saw me taking a picture after a game. Apparently, I'm not using natural light to my advantage."

"My photos have improved since he told me my left is my best side." Calder strikes a pose, sucking in his cheeks like a supermodel strutting down the runway.

I chuckle and Axel groans as Calder mimes flipping his hair over his shoulder. The more time I spend with Calder and his teammates, the more I appreciate their camaraderie. They harass each other and tease like brothers, but their affection is clear. It's been nice to see how they support each other off the ice.

Sawyer returns, and I'm able to complete the final adjustments without issue. Within an hour Axel and Sawyer are gone, arguing over whose turn it was to buy the other dinner, and I'm on the couch cuddled into Calder's side, tucked under his arm, wearing an old sweatshirt and sweatpants of his that are too big on me but are cozy and smell faintly of him. His fingertips trail along my skin at my wrist, triggering an eruption of goosebumps. Head on his shoulder, I sigh into his neck. "This is nice."

"We'll have less of this once the season begins." His throat bobs. "Will you be okay with that?"

I sit up and gaze at the lip he's working between his teeth. "What are you asking?"

"I don't know... I've seen a lot of relationships end because of the stress of the schedule and travel." Lines form on his forehead, and the worried glances he's sent me since training camp for the Power began last week now make sense. With him busy with camp and playing three preseason games within the last six days, I've gotten a taste of being a hockey boyfriend. There are two more games to go, starting tomorrow, and both are away games, so after tonight I won't get to see him for three days.

My heart accelerates to overdrive. Although we've been dating exclusively since the awards show, we haven't had the *relationship* talk. "So we're in a relationship?"

His mouth goes slack, then his eyes narrow, and he tugs me to his lap until I'm straddling him. The lip he was worrying now softly grazes my neck. "In case I haven't made it clear, you're the guy for me."

"You've made it extremely clear." I comb my fingers through his soft hair, tousling it until he looks like he's been thoroughly sexed up. Which is my favorite look on him. "And for the sake of clarity, there is no other person I'd rather be with."

His smile is the sun and every star in the sky combined, and I bask in its radiance. "I love you."

"I love you, too." My voice cracks and I blink back moisture. "I've wanted to tell you, but I was afraid it was too soon."

His large hands cup my face. "Babe, I've been in love with you since the first time I saw you in suspenders."

"That was our first date."

"And I've loved you since then." His kiss is honey with sugar sprinkled on top, and the unyielding hardness pressed against me is sweaty nights with unending pleasure. "You'll be okay with my schedule?"

"Probably not."

His expression morphs from dazzling to dejected in a nanosecond.

Smoothing the creases between his brows with the pad of my thumb, I then press my lips to the corner of his downturned mouth. "I'll miss you and miss not being with you almost every day. So, no, I'm not okay with your schedule. *However*, we'll text, and there are always video calls... That could be sexy." I waggle my eyebrows, and he squeezes my bottom, his eyes darkening. "We'll figure it out and make it work."

He bolts from the couch and I let out a startled yelp as I travel up with him, wrapping my legs around his waist as he stands, arms secure around me. Striding to the bedroom, he presses his mouth to mine in a firm kiss as I hold on tight. When he disengages his mouth from mine, his glow is back. "We're celebrating our official couplehood."

"Had I known there'd be a celebration, I would have insisted on confirming our relationship status months ago." I kiss the dimpled chin I can't get enough of.

He drops me onto the bed and is over me before I finish bouncing. "I love you. Damn, I like saying that."

"I hope you plan on saying it a lot, because I plan on telling you I love you every chance I get." Flooded with bliss that his man is mine, I cup his gorgeous face and kiss him.

His knuckles stroke my cheek. "Good, because you're my perfect fit."

"Yeah." Heart full, I catch his hand and press a kiss into his palm. "You were tailored for me."

Coming Soon

Behind the Mask

Philadelphia Power Hockey series

Ryder Stone loves making people happy. He's worked hard to turn Striker, the mascot for the Philadelphia Power, into a beloved fixture and fan favorite. Being Striker has given Ryder his livelihood, his friend group, and his best friend Sawyer, who's been Ryder's biggest cheerleader in their nearly decade-long friendship. But now, he's seeing Sawyer in a new light. A romantic one.

Starting goalie for the Power, Sawyer Garcia, is a dog lover passionate about pet adoption, painting, hockey, and his friendships. The veteran hockey player has spent the last nine years in Philly, and his best friend Ryder is the reason the city feels like home. He's a planner, but doesn't know what to do about the feelings he's developed for Ryder, the most important person in his world.

One impulsive kiss changes everything and turns their worlds upside down. They've always clicked so well together and know each other better than anyone. Crossing the line from best friends to lovers has the potential to ruin their friendship, but also to give them more than they ever thought possible.

https://www.shelleyandmer.com/behind-the-mask

·❤·❤·❤·❤·❤·

Visit our website for our full book list, excerpts, and more:
https://www.shelleyandmer.com/

Sign up for Susan and Chantal's reader newsletter:
https://www.shelleyandmer.com/newsletter

Also By Susan & Chantal

Love & Rugby

Spiral

Spark

Smolder

Shine

Surprise

Swoon

Love & Rugby: Season of Love

Savor

Seduce

Stay

Philadelphia Power

Against the Rush

Over the Top

Behind the Mask

Also By Susan

Philadelphia Frenzy

Mad Scramble

Buffalo Bedlam

Skating on Chance

Holding on Tight

Scoring Slater

Bliss Bakery

Sugar Crush

Falling series

Falling Faster

For Susan's full book list, please go to:

https://www.susanscottshelley.com/books

Also By Chantal

Absolving Ash

·♥·♥·♥·♥·♥·

Love in Philly
Where I Belong

·♥·♥·♥·♥·♥·

For Chantal's full book list, please go to:
https://www.chantalmer.com/books-1

About Susan

USA TODAY bestselling author Susan Scott Shelley writes romances with heat and heart that celebrate love without limits. Enormous mugs of coffee and tea make her happy, as does reading romance novels and binging episodes of her favorite British TV shows. Susan also works as a professional voiceover artist, and while she's definitely a city girl, she likes being out in nature as often as possible. A fan of mythology, word games, and hockey, she lives in Philadelphia with her husband and has yet to meet a plant she hasn't wanted to take home.

Visit her website for her full book list, excerpts, and more:
   http://www.susanscottshelley.com

About Chantal

Chantal Mer never set out to write books. Yet here she is, and she's having a blast. Happily ever afters for everyone makes her heart sing. When she's not writing, Chantal can be found walking her adorable dog, going to musical theater with her daughter, observing the night sky with her husband and his telescope, and learning about the latest advances in video games with her son. Give her a book and a glass of wine and she's in her happy place. Chantal lives outside of Philadelphia with her husband, two teens, and her sweet pup, Miss Toffee, and her big orange tabby cat, Simba.

To keep up to date with Chantal, check out her website.
https://chantalmer.com/

Sign up for Chantal's reader newsletter:
https://chantalmer.com/newsletters/